Who delivered the deadly kung fu blow that nearly ended Dick Harrington's life? And why are the kids at the Galaxy Games video arcade acting like robots, playing as if they can't stop? When James Budd tries to find out, someone tries to kill him. But James will not be stopped—for he and Honey Mack are determined to solve THE MYSTERY OF GALAXY GAMES.

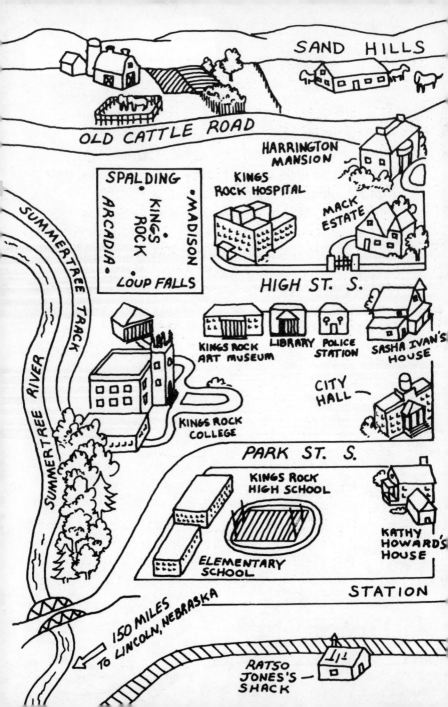

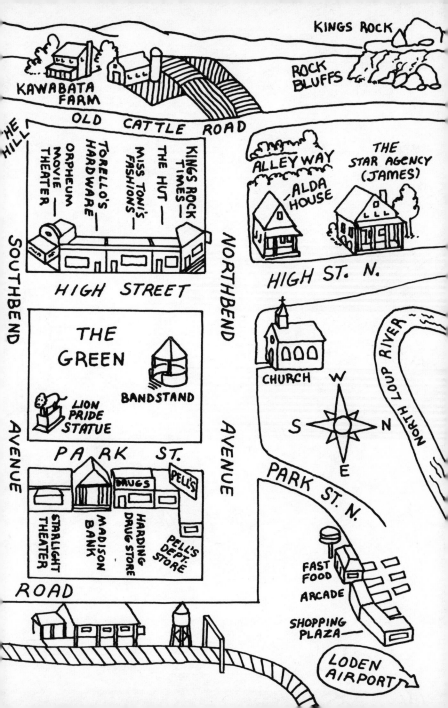

THE MYSTERY OF
GALAXY
GAMES

By Dale Carlson

**Illustrated by
Tom LaPadula**

**Cover illustration by
Chuck Liese**

A GOLDEN BOOK • NEW YORK

WESTERN PUBLISHING COMPANY, INC.,
RACINE, WISCONSIN 53404

For Ray Fisher
Part James
Part Charlie
Part of me

Contents

THE MYSTERY OF
GALAXY
GAMES

CHAPTER ONE

Get James Budd!

The body beside the Harrington pool seemed dead.

"Get James," whispered Mrs. Harrington over her son's body. "Get James Budd! That young man will know what to do. He always does."

James Budd, at sixteen, was not only the adopted son of the famous private detective Sam Star, but his right-hand man. After school, during vacations, and whenever Sam was away on a case, James worked for or took over for Sam. People in Kings Rock, all over Nebraska, and in a lot of other states as well, were as used to seeing James Budd on a case as Sam Star.

"James is a born fixer," Sam always said. "He can't leave well enough, or anything else, alone. And if there's no trouble," Sam would add, "leave it to James, he'll make it."

But today the Harringtons, one of Kings Rock's richest and most prominent families, had real trouble. Dick Harrington's body lay pale and still beside the empty swimming pool in the dappled sunlight of the early-November afternoon.

"Sam Star is out of town, working on a case," said Mrs. Harrington to her husband, through trembling tears. "Get James Budd, dear, please," she repeated.

"We'll be right there," said James, when Mr. Harrington called.

Five minutes later, James left the home on High Street North that housed himself, Sam, and the Star Agency. He drove down past the Green to Southbend Avenue, and west onto the Hill. The Hill was where the rich of Kings Rock lived. James made a stop first at the Mack Estate, next door to the Harringtons.

A moment later, a familiar Kings Rock sight appeared in the circular driveway in front of the Harrington mansion — James Budd and his detective partner, girl, and friend, Honey Mack. James and Honey pulled up in an old, specially reconstructed red Firebird — an inescapable and unbeatable threesome.

As James Budd crossed the yard toward the pool, he was aware that he and Honey, whose name came from the dark gold of her waist-long hair, made a good-looking couple. James himself was dark, with a strong-jawed, clean-cut face, wide, dark eyes, and black hair. He was not violent by nature, but he was a stubborn fighter for what he felt was right. He bore a two-inch scar on his sun-tanned forehead from an old fight. James knew basic judo and karate, the arts of unarmed self-defense, in case of necessity. He was an all-round athlete, got straight A's in school, and he liked to dress well.

"Handsome devil, and you know it," Honey always teased. "I spend my life with a base-ball bat, slugging girls away from you."

"When you're born independent, you get to make anything out of yourself you like," James always answered.

Being "born independent" was the only way he ever spoke of being orphaned by parents he never knew and adopted out of an orphanage at the age of four by Sam Star. Sam, Charlie Alda, electronics genius and James's best friend in their junior class at Kings Rock High School, and Honey Mack, the prettiest girl, fastest runner, and fastest driver of any class anywhere, were James's family now.

As James and Honey approached, Mrs. Harrington looked up at the two tall, slim visitors, dressed alike in gleaming white warm-up suits.

"Thank heavens you're here," she said, gazing up at James as if he were a shining knight who had just ridden in on the wind.

As Mr. Harrington bent over his wife, Mrs. Harrington bent over her son. Kneeling beside the inert body, she touched the silky blond hair, the pale forehead.

James looked down at the body outlined against the ground, then gently guided Mrs. Harrington away.

"Let me have a look at Dick," he said, his voice as gentle as his touch.

Dick Harrington was in James and Honey's class in school. His parents had made something of a spoiled snob of him. But if he wasn't exactly James's type, neither did James like the idea that someone had hurt him.

And someone *had* hurt Dick Harrington. Someone had hurt him very badly. James's fingers touched Dick's head, traveled the length of Dick's back, stomach, chest, arms, legs. No bones broken, but what of internal injuries?

The site of the blow was nearly invisible.

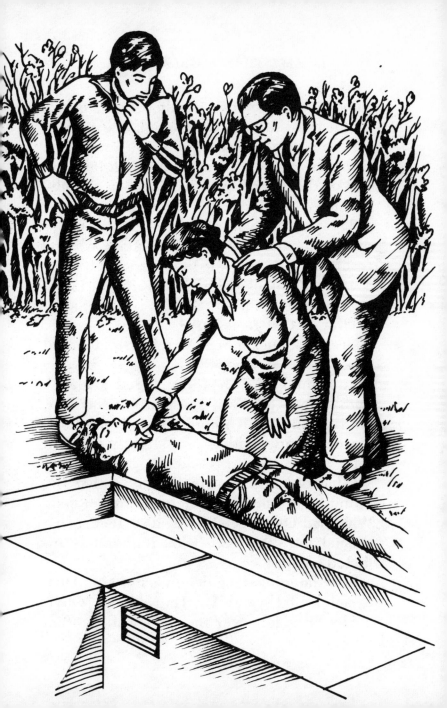

James himself spotted it only because of two elements in his own background. The first was his knowledge of basic judo and karate. The second was the stuff Sam had taught James in the medical examiner's lab next to the city morgue.

The faint bruise over Dick Harrington's midsection, James was almost certain, was the result of a killer blow to the spleen.

"Better call an ambulance, sir," said James to Mr. Harrington.

"But is that necessary? Couldn't we just take care of Dick here?" Mrs. Harrington said quickly.

Too quickly? James exchanged a glance with Honey to see if she had noticed Mrs. Harrington's swift interference. Honey had noticed, and nodded just slightly back to James.

What did Mrs. Harrington know that she didn't want known publicly about her son? What had Dick been involved in, that such a specialized blow had been deliberately inflicted on him?

"But James is right, dear. We must get Dick to a hospital," said Mr. Harrington. "Obviously, Dick fell over the pool wall. I often wondered about this low pool wall being dangerous."

In his grief, Mr. Harrington had begun to ramble. But he pulled his thoughts together and went on. "You wanted James to see Dick first. And now James is here, and he feels just as I do. I'll go call for the ambulance right away."

As Mr. Harrington went toward the white-columned portico of the mansion, Mrs. Harrington exchanged a long, long look with James Budd.

"We're trying to read each other's minds," James whispered to Honey.

But all Mrs. Harrington would say aloud was, "Is he dead? Is my son dead, James?"

James had already covered Dick's upper body with his own white jacket. He lifted the jacket slightly to point to the bruise on Dick's upper left abdomen, just beneath the ribs.

"He's in shock. There is some evidence of hemorrhage, internal bleeding," said James. "I think the spleen's been ruptured."

Mrs. Harrington gasped.

"It's been caused by a sudden, severe blow to the abdomen," said James. "And I don't see how it could have been an accident."

"Will he die?" Mrs. Harrington asked, full of pain.

"Sam told me once, on another case, that a ruptured spleen has to be surgically removed right away," James answered. He didn't add — *or it's fatal*.

Honey supported a half-fainting Mrs. Harrington as the ambulance siren was heard, and as the paramedics came to transport her son to emergency surgery at Kings Rock Hospital. The Harringtons went with Dick in the ambulance.

James drove Honey back to the Star Agency, where both he and Honey were paid to keep Sam's records, organize his files, answer his telephone, and fill in where they could for Sam Star himself.

"On this one, we need Sam," said James.

He parked the Firebird in the garage and took the porch steps in a single easy motion. To the left of the front hall was Sam and James's large, leather-and-brass living room. To the right were the Star Agency's offices. James went through the waiting room into the back office to the telephone. Honey picked up the mail in the front office.

"James," the honey-haired girl called softly.

"Yes?" James answered.

"Is Dick going to die from that blow, surgery or not?"

"Probably," answered James.

"Oh, no," Honey whispered. "Oh, James, no!"

James came out of the inner office to take a piece of notepaper out of Honey's shaking hands. It said, in printed block letters, with no identifying signature: JAMES BUDD, STAY OFF THIS CASE OR THE SAME BLOW WILL COME TO YOU. BE WARNED, YOUR LIFE TOO WILL BLEED AWAY.

In that moment of stillness, as James read, the silhouette of a man appeared outside the curtained front window.

CHAPTER TWO

Get Sam!

"Drop," said James.

Honey flattened on the floor next to James until the silhouette passed from view. James didn't want the message carrier outside to see their outlines, as they had seen his. But the moment the man was gone from the window, James sprang to his feet.

Followed by Honey, he raced across the front hall from the offices to the private half, through the living room, and back toward the kitchen. Through the kitchen window, James saw their visitor run for the alleyway behind the house on High Street North and leap into a black sedan. He couldn't see the license plate number.

"LCP-435," Honey said behind James a moment later.

She had raced out to the alleyway and back

almost before James had noted the car's make and year.

"Girl, you are really fast on your feet," said James, grinning at Honey and pulling her to him for a hug they didn't have time to linger in.

In a single motion, they pulled apart and raced out to the garage. James gunned the Firebird and pressed a button on the remote control panel Charlie Alda had installed when he modified the '71 Pontiac engine for James. The button opened the special back entrance to the garage. James leaped the Firebird through and into the alleyway, made a right onto High Street North, and spotted the black Chevy going south.

The Green formed the center of Kings Rock, with its bandstand and its statue of the Lion Pride. From the Green sprang all of Kings Rock's streets, Northbend and Southbend Avenues going east and west, High Street and Park Street going north and south. James's mental map kept all fixtures available to sort through. To the northwest, at the foot of the Sand Hills, was Rock Bluffs, with the rock plateau called Kings Rock that gave the town its name. To the northwest were the shopping mall, the arcades, junk food row, and Loden Airport. To the east was the railroad, to the south of Kings Rock was Summertree River flowing into Middle Loup River, and to the west of town stretched the farms, the corn- fields, and cattle herds of Nebraska.

James always needed to replay various de- tails of his mental maps. "I hate being lost, or losing anything," James always said.

The black Chevy was now heading east on Southbend Avenue in the direction of the rail- road tracks. It was going just at the speed limit.

"He's seen us following him," said James. "But he doesn't dare move out faster."

"He doesn't want to get stopped," said Honey. "Do you think he's headed for the six- forty to Lincoln?" Lincoln, Nebraska, was 150 miles southeast of Kings Rock. "He could sure get lost in Lincoln."

James stepped on the accelerator, to make sure he didn't lose the man in the black sedan who had just gunned his car across Station Road. The two cars swerved almost simulta- neously up toward the railroad station, each now fully aware of the other's intentions. The older man in the black Chevy wanted to catch the six-forty out of town. The younger man in

the red Firebird wanted him not to catch the evening train or anything else to get out of town.

"James, be careful," yelled Honey, "or you'll bloody well do us in as well as him."

James raced at the Chevy one more time to cut it off, coming dangerously near, then pulling over at an angle in front of the oncoming driver.

"Blast him," swore James under his breath.

As James's tires screeched to cut off the Chevy, the Chevy stopped. The messenger leaped from the passenger seat of the car and raced along the railway track toward the station.

James and Honey were after him. As the three raced toward the station from the south, the Lincoln train was pulling in from the north.

"We've got to cut him off or he's going to make that train," James shouted over the train's roar.

Honey's hair streamed behind her like an Olympic runner's banner. Even in a crisis, James couldn't help but flash an admiring smile at the beautiful, slim girl running by his side.

He shouted at her one more time. "You're how girls ought to look," he said, his voice carrying over the whistle of the train.

"Maniac," Honey shouted fondly back. "Tend to business."

The messenger who was their current business was slowing down slightly, judging by the narrowing gap between him and his pursuers. James and Honey picked up their pace. So did the driver of the black Chevrolet.

"He's in good shape," called James.

"Considering how good we are, he's incredible," Honey shouted back. "Specially trained, do you think?"

James decided to conserve breath. It suddenly occurred to him that this man might be more than a messenger. He might be the karate expert who had delivered the blow to Dick Harrington, and he just might be the instrument of a similar blow to James's own midsection, as promised by the threatening letter he'd just received.

James let out his long, athletic stride as far as possible and with a last spurt reached for the train. The train, however, had by then picked up too much speed. James was too late, unless he wanted to break a leg with a split-second leap. The man he and Honey had been chasing had not been too late. His lead of a few seconds had made it possible for him to get aboard. Whether he had broken anything doing so, James could not yet know.

"Next?" asked Honey, when the two of them had walked back to the Firebird and, still breathing hard, climbed in.

"To the hospital, to see about Dick Harrington and to call Sam," said James.

As James turned on the ignition, Honey pushed back a fallen lock of thick black hair. Because it was Honey's hand, James smiled. Anyone else's, he'd have bitten off at the shoulder.

James drove back along Southbend, past Park Street South, where Kings Rock High was turning on its lights for evening activities, to High Street South, where the white buildings of Kings Rock Hospital took on a soft blue tint as night began to fall.

James had passes to everywhere, thanks to Sam Star. He got Honey and himself past all the nurses' stations and up onto the intensive care unit floor, where critically ill patients were monitored round the clock.

"First Sam," said James.

He dialed the special number Sam had left him in case of emergency.

"James?" said Sam, coming directly onto the line. "What's up?"

James described the past few hours, and the characters and incidents that had filled them, to his adoptive father and boss, Sam Star, Private Investigator. He could all but see the thin, wiry, sharp-eyed man, who didn't hit, didn't use guns, and who was the smartest man James had ever known. He could all but see Sam push back the gray felt hat he always wore. He could all but hear his mind decide which were the important questions to answer.

"Find out what Mrs. Harrington knows about her son's activities. Find out why she wanted you there first, before calling either the police or the ambulance or their private physician. Find out who delivered that killer blow to Dick Harrington and why," said Sam in the cool, even voice James knew and loved.

"Is that all?" James answered, in the cool, even voice Sam knew and loved just as much.

"As a matter of fact, it isn't," said Sam. "I want you to go up to the Wolf Electronics Plant. Mr. Wolf left a message for me that some electronics parts have been disappearing. Make sure he understands we charge three hundred dollars a day plus expenses, then take down his details."

"Right," said James.

"Be home by Friday," said Sam. "Love to Honey. Not to worry about the threatening letter. Good-by."

James smiled at the silent receiver before hanging up. He had known Sam Star for twelve years and had yet to figure out why he talked into the telephone as if he were sending a telegram.

"He sends you his love. He didn't ask whether Dick was alive or dead," said James.

"Maybe he knew," said Honey.

"Good thought," said James. "Do we?"

CHAPTER THREE

A Wolf in Leather Clothing

Valentine Wolf wore black leather pants. They were as sleek as the rest of her, with her long black hair and the green cat eyes that glittered like her smile.

As she opened the door to her father's offices at the Wolf Electronics Plant, she smiled that glittery smile as she spoke.

"James? James Budd?" Valentine's movements were lithe and smooth as James followed her through the waiting room and down a long hall, past closed doors toward the heavy door at the far end.

The carpeting, the gilt furniture, the gleaming chandeliers, all seemed rather rich for ordinary offices. Intuitively, James wondered if more went on in these rooms than the mere running of a single electronics parts factory.

"Nice pants," said James. He had to make

some kind of remark, since Valentine was making such an effort to flirt with him.

"Thank you, James," said Valentine from under a flutter of eyelashes. "Not something you'd see at Kings Rock High, true?"

"True," admitted James, knowing Valentine meant her entire self, not just the expensive black leather.

Valentine Wolf didn't go to school. Valentine had special tutors. Valentine's father didn't want his daughter mixing with the local children, he said, as it wouldn't do for his daughter to get too attached to any one place or any one group of people. The Wolf Electronics Plants were a national network, and Volpone Wolf and his daughter Valentine moved yearly from one plant to the next. If there was a Mrs. Wolf, no one had ever heard of her, and Valentine acted as hostess whenever her father entertained.

It was Valentine who had answered the telephone earlier that day, when James had called to request an interview with Mr. Wolf.

"Is this a social call, James?" Valentine wanted to know. She opened the heavy door at the end of the hall.

"Not really," said James. Your father called Sam Star to report the theft of some electronics parts.He asked us to investigate, see what we could come up with. I do Sam's preliminary work when he's out of town."

Valentine was visibly impressed.

"James Budd to see you, daddy," she said.

The man who rose to greet James had a middle European accent, thick, overhanging brows, dark, flashing eyes, a swarthy face, and white teeth that James could easily imagine clenching a knife.

Those cunning eyes raked James's face and person as Mr. Wolf asked, "And how is our friend Dick Harrington? What news from the hospital?"

It was now up to him, James knew, to betray nothing. He must ask no questions that might connect the blow Dick had received, the man in the black sedan, the threatening letter he himself had gotten, and the reasons a private investigator was called instead of the police to track down the missing electronics parts. It wasn't easy, but James did his best to look bland as he answered. "Still touch and go, sir. Thank you for asking. They've removed the spleen, naturally. They still don't know the extent of the hemorrhaging."

How does that man know about Dick, blast it?

A newspaper on Volpone Wolf's desk caught James's eye. The story was on the front page.

Boy, can I get stupid, James thought.

But then Mr. Wolf smiled, as if he had followed every inch of James's train of thought.

I was right, thought James. *He may have picked up the story in the* Kings Rock Times. *But he still has his own reasons for asking about Dick Harrington's health.*

In response to the gesture and canine smile of his host, James sat down smoothly in the armchair opposite Mr. Wolf.

"What will you have, James?" Mr. Wolf asked. "You must be hungry after school." He sounded as if he were talking to a small child.

It wasn't easy, ever, for anyone, to put James Budd in his place. James crossed one neat, gray-flannel-trousered leg over the other and said, "I'll have coffee, please. And actually, I've just come from my Chinese Shaolin karate class, where I was working with the sunfist technique. You know, of course, that it was a sunfist blow to Dick's spleen that may be killing him now."

James's voice was quiet, his eyes watchful as he flicked a piece of lint from his gray flannel lap.

"Why should I know a thing like that?" said Mr. Wolf. "The *Times* mentioned nothing of what caused the boy's injury."

He handed James a coffee cup from the tray Valentine had just brought in. Valentine looked at James sideways, quickly.

Did she know something that wasn't being said? James wondered just how involved Valentine was in her father's affairs.

"And now — about my affairs?" said Mr. Wolf.

"Of course," said James. "Have you a list of the parts that are missing?"

"Naturally," said Mr. Wolf. He handed James a typewritten list.

"When were the parts stolen?" James asked.

"My foreman began to notice that things were missing last week. At first we thought the factory hands were having a spate of carelessness. It happens, you know. But this morning, when more parts had disappeared over the weekend, it became obvious."

"What became obvious?" said James.

"That someone has been systematically robbing the electronics plant," said Mr. Wolf.

James had been glancing over the list. The parts and components listed made no sense to him. He'd show the list later to Charlie Alda.

"If there's a system, we'll find it," said James. "The parts will add up to something, something someone is building. Whatever is being built will give us the first clue to whoever is doing the building. And whoever is doing the building will lead us to whoever is planning the thefts."

"Very clever," said Mr. Wolf.

The glitter of appreciation in the flashing eyes, so like the glitter in the eyes of his beautiful young daughter, gave James the idea that as much as Volpone Wolf wanted to catch the thief, he admired the cunning of a good thief as well.

"You'll hear from us soon," said James. "I'll start on this right away, and Sam himself will be back on Friday to follow up."

A look passed between Volpone Wolf and Valentine. She not only showed James back down the corridor to the waiting room, but escorted him unnecessarily all the way out of the factory.

James met all kinds of girls working with Sam Star. He would have to be deaf, dumb, and blind not to notice that he seemed to have a chemical effect on them. But in this case, James wasn't absolutely certain of Valentine's motive in flirting with him.

"James?" she purred, as they reached the plant's front door.

"Yes, Valentine?" said James.

He managed to hold the factory door open another long moment as he examined a general blueprint of the plant, complete with assembly-line details, that was tacked to the wall. He managed to examine it even while Valentine, with a single sinuous movement, curved in against James and lifted her face for a kiss.

Was it because James was so devastatingly handsome?

Or was it because, in the interest of her father's interests, she wanted to stop James from concentrating on the factory plans, maps, and lists on the wall?

James was not going to find out — not that afternoon, anyway.

From nowhere, Honey Mack appeared. James could hear the roar of Honey's blue Honda CB125S motorcycle even before she rounded the corner. She was off the bike and yanking her helmet from the flowing, honey hair three seconds before Valentine made contact for her kiss.

"Hello, everybody," Honey sang out.

Valentine's smile glittered future promises before she disappeared behind the factory door.

"James," said Honey, "I wouldn't want you to feel deprived."

She gave him the kiss herself.

"I don't," said James. "Feel deprived, that is. You're all the girl I need, Honey mine."

That much was true. James meant what he said. Under his cool competence, James needed someone, needed Honey, to share his life, his love, his passion for excitement. Other girls were pretty. Honey Mack was his.

He rode pillion behind Honey as she

headed south. She went past the power plant along Old Cattle Road, which skirted downtown Kings Rock to the west. Both of them loved the flying speed of the bike.

They loved it so much, they almost didn't hear the roaring engine of the big, black Harley doing seventy behind them. By the time Honey glimpsed the goggled rider in her rearview mirror and twisted her handlebars to swerve from the road, it was almost too late.

CHAPTER FOUR

The Threat of Ratso

"You were where? The rider did what? Honey swerved down where? You're trying to get yourselves killed, and I'll lose the best friends I've got."

Charlie Alda's rapid-fire questions and gloomy conclusion could be heard across the entire span of the Kings Rock High School gym, where, on Wednesday, James and Honey were relating the previous day's experiences. The whole Kings Rock track team, of which James was all-round star and Honey the star sprinter, was doing warm-up exercises on the gym floor. They had a meet with Arcadia High in two weeks, and they didn't want to lose. Winning meets, as James reminded them, was one way of getting out of town oftener.

Charlie's gloomy panic, however, attracted attention. Charlie adored James, and whenever James's escapes were narrower than usual, the cute owlish face under the mop of blond, curly hair and behind the horn-rimmed glasses would begin to perspire. Charlie's gloom was also, he would explain, due to the crowded living conditions of this planet, which he was going to devote his entire electronics genius to leaving, with a view to locating another. Living with five young brothers and sisters contributed to his zeal.

At the moment, however, his energy was directed at James.

"Why do you get into these things? And if you must, why can't you get into them in your car? I've built enough stuff into that car to protect you, from bullet-proof windows to automatic locking systems," said Charlie, "to say nothing of CB with a direct line to Police Chief Adams, and the loudest siren in the state."

"The Harley came up behind us not too far from the Wolf Electronics Plant," said James. "But that doesn't necessarily mean there's any connection between the Wolfs and that killer on the motorcycle. I mean, I can't think of anything we said or saw to scare Mr. Wolf into wanting me dead."

"What about those plans, those maps, James?" said Honey.

"I suppose it's possible I saw something I wasn't supposed to see," said James. "But those plans meant nothing to me. Don't forget the threatening letter delivered by the man in the black sedan, Honey. It's far more likely that goggled rider had something to do with the Dick Harrington case."

"What threatening letter?" Charlie Alda was mopping his glasses, and with this new scare, his voice was nearly a howl.

That did it. The whole track team crowded around James and Honey, asking questions. James and Honey already had something of a reputation for being involved in Sam Star's cases, and their friends liked being in on the excitement. Besides, they were all concerned about Dick, still in the hospital, still neither dead nor wholly alive.

A tall, beautiful black girl pushed her way through the pack and threw her arms around Honey.

"You all right?" Kathy Howard demanded.

Kathy was Honey's closest friend. She had three passions in life: being gorgeous; falling

in love often; and astrophysics. Kathy Howard's idea of heaven was to be up in a NASA Spacelab someday, along with five men, wearing something chic in a spacesuit.

"We're all right," Honey answered.

"Honey was wonderful," James said. "When she caught sight of that goggled horror behind us, she swerved those handlebars as if they were on ball bearings. She took us right off Old Cattle Road into that ditch near the Kawabata farm."

"When James felt what I was doing," Honey said, "he leaned forward and took control of the leap, or we'd have ended up in that ditch with the Honda on top of us instead of underneath. Anyway, by then there were cars coming, so the Harley couldn't turn back for another try at us without being seen. He just took off down Old Cattle Road and was gone."

"You're onto something somebody really doesn't want you onto," said Tad Kawabata. "You'd better come for extra martial arts lessons from my father."

The Kawabata family had come from Japan to live among the cornfields of Nebraska. But they had brought with them Zen Buddhism, with its meditation, its beautiful attention to the details of life, its painting, tea ceremony, archery, and the practice of judo, kung fu, and karate.

"We're all coming over next week anyway, Tad," said Clara Rand, Kings Rock High School's best artist.

Joe Levy, football hero, and Jilly Bruce, the school's best actress and president of the Drama Club, agreed with a nod. "Mr. Kawabata is teaching us some calligraphy for the decorations for next year's Rock," Jilly said. The Rock was the senior high school dance in October. This year's dance had been wonderful. Plans for the next one were already under way.

"Fine," said Tad. "I'll tell my father to add some special karate to the calligraphy lessons. And I'm not altogether kidding, either, James. You really sound as if you're up against something heavy this time."

"What's the matter, big James come up with something he can't handle for a change?" came a voice that could only be described as mean.

The owner of the voice, Ratso Jones, came sidling up from the back of the gym. He was followed as usual by his sidekicks, Tom and

Sharky. Ratso, who was skinny, narrow-eyed, and always wore leather, had a mission in life. Whenever he could, he tried to trip up James Budd.

"Well, Ratso," said James. He leaned tolerantly back against the gymnasium stage. "Anything new in your life? A sunfist blow, a black sedan, an oversized Harley?"

"I don't know anything about them things," said Ratso belligerently.

"I didn't think you did," said James.

"So what are you trying to do, get me in trouble?" said Ratso. He moved a step forward. Tom and Sharky moved a step forward behind him.

"Not if you stay clear of the case Honey and I are working on for Sam," said James. He still felt and looked unruffled.

"Get in James's way, you got trouble," said Honey.

Honey often protected James faster than he needed protection, and even when he needed no protection at all. She knew a little about karate and the white snake and the monkey knee herself. But what Honey Mack did best was glare. From her greater height, she glared down at Ratso now.

"I appreciate your effort, Honey," whispered James. "But I think he's more noise than threat at the moment."

With a rude gesture and without another word, Ratso backed off with his gang and left the gym.

"It's his nuisance value I worry about," said Charlie. "He's made messes for you before, James, that nearly wrecked your investigations. He's a born saboteur, a screw-up, you know?"

"I know," said James. "I've lived with Ratso around my neck since I was in the second grade."

"Pay attention to what Charlie's saying," said Kathy. "Where you go, Honey goes, and where Honey goes, I worry. And we've all noticed Ratso Jones has been hauling again."

Ratso's father was the stationmaster. He had turned over to Ratso and his friends an abandoned railroad shack not far from the station. They used it variously as clubhouse, escape hole, and warehouse. Whatever any of them scavenged ended up in Ratso Jones's shack. Sometimes the hauling escalated, and deals were made. When they were eight, the deals were in baseball cards and aggies. Eight years later, the deals were less cute, less innocent, and often less legal.

"Any idea what?" said James.

"We'll check," said Charlie, Tad, and Joe.

"Thanks," said James.

Everybody went back to warm-up exercises. With James and Honey in their midst, everyone's energy rose.

That was Wednesday.

By Friday, there was nearly no energy at all in some of them.

CHAPTER FIVE

Brains and Games

By Friday also, Sam Star was due home.
James woke on Friday morning looking
forward to the day. By four o'clock that afternoon, Sam would be putting down at Loden
Airport, northeast of Kings Rock. By four
o'clock, James would have his adoptive father,
friend, and employer back — all of whom he
needed to ask questions.

In the meantime, he had a full day before
him. On the agenda were school, his daily
workout, tracing the list of missing factory
parts for Mr. Wolf, and an early tea with Mrs.
Harrington to ask a few more questions about
Dick and his activities. School, luckily, was
only a half-day today.

James removed Band-Aid, a big, affectionate black Labrador retriever from next door,
who spent most of his nights sprawled on

James's feet, from his bed. Next, James fell to the floor and, while Band-Aid licked his face, did the twenty pushups that got his motor running for the morning.

"Ban, push off, will you?" said James, laughing and heading for the shower. But two dog biscuits accompanied James's words, and Band-Aid hung around.

His black hair shining and combed, James chose a white shirt, tan gabs, and a navy blazer under his camel's-hair coat for the day. The dark eyes in his mirror reflected approval. James had discovered long ago that his youthfulness as a private investigator was more acceptable in conservative dress.

"Anyway," as Honey often said of him, "James is a loner — sociable, but a loner. He doesn't really care what everybody else does, thinks, or wears. Only his own opinion of himself, and maybe Sam's, matters to James."

And as James always answered playfully when Honey got descriptive on him, "A lot you know!"

But Honey was right. Honey generally was. And since she was the one who wrote up their cases, often for publication in the *Kings Rock*

Times, James had a healthy respect for her analyses of people and events.

The Firebird hummed down High Street, made a right onto Southbend Avenue to pick up Honey as it did most mornings, turned back down Southbend, and made another right onto Park Street South and down to Kings Rock High. Honey, elegant in a white wool coat, did a model's half-turn for James's cool appraisal as they stepped from the red car. She would join him later at Mrs. Harrington's, and James wanted her looking quiet, capable, and, above all, trustworthy.

"Good," said James. "Three o'clock at the Harrington house, then? I have some things to do first. I'll meet you there."

Honey nodded and spun off to her advanced English course. James headed for his biopsychology class, where he could occasionally persuade their teacher, Dr. Hannah Bick, to discuss criminal psychopathology with them.

James's first stop after school was the school lab. He wanted to go over the list of electronics parts with Charlie Alda.

Charlie looked up from a row of flasks, test tubes, wires, batteries, control boxes, and assorted minute mechanisms unrecognizable to James. He checked over Mr. Wolf's list of missing parts without a word.

"Assembled properly into a computer, those parts could be used to send audio-visual messages not detectable in the ordinary sensory range," said Charlie.

"Now speak English," said James.

Charlie peered owlishly through the horn-rimmed glasses at his friend and grinned.

"Like just because you can't see certain things, it doesn't mean they aren't there. Electronic equipment can be organized to send out messages your eyes and ears can't make out in the normal way," Charlie explained. "The brain can receive sounds and images in a subliminal way, though, and translate and store the messages — even obey them. You can use a variety of methods, from filmstrips to audio video cassettes, all doctored to blip hypnotic messages too fast for the conscious eye and ear, but not too fast for the subconscious."

"Sneaky," said James.

"Anything goes, trying to reach the otherwise unreachable," said Charlie cheerfully.

"I don't know about that," said James. His face was thoughtful. "I don't think the means

and the ends are so separate, Charlie. Anyway, thanks. Transmitting parts? Recorder parts, you say, right?"

"Right," said Charlie. "Here, I'll sketch a few for you quickly, and diagram how they might work."

Half an hour later, James left Charlie, carrying some very useful drawings in his pocket.

As James climbed into his Firebird, he felt his usual pleasure at seeing things fall into a pattern. The fact that all the stolen parts from the Wolf Electronics Plant fell into a definite category gave direction to his investigation. James liked order. And this tidy report would please Sam.

But only in events did he like order. As he drove up the hill to the Harrington Estate, James preferred the wild, rambling clouds, wind-driven across the wide Nebraska sky, to the tidy flower beds and clipped hedges of the Harrington grounds.

Honey and Mrs. Harrington were in the large main drawing room waiting for James. Honey sat, relaxed, on a love seat near the fireplace, holding a teacup. Mrs. Harrington stood, clinging a little too dramatically, James thought, to the silk hangings at the French doors overlooking the gardens.

"Mrs. Harrington?"

"There you are, James. Thank goodness. Have you been to the hospital?"

"I called," said James.

"Then you know. Dick has had his operation, but they're still worried," said Mrs. Harrington, touching a bit of handkerchief lace to her eyes. "He's not even allowed visitors."

"I know," said James. "That's not the best news, Mrs. Harrington. I had hoped he'd be really better. I'm so sorry."

James came forward and led Mrs. Harrington to the love seat opposite Honey. He kept her hand in his own as they sat down.

"And now I want you to help us, Mrs. Harrington," said James. "I know how upset you've been since Monday afternoon, but you've got to help us if we're going to find out what happened to Dick and who attacked him. Please, tell us anything, anything at all unusual about Dick in the past weeks. All we've noticed at school is that he's been coming late and leaving early, as if he's had something else on his mind, something else to do."

"Can you tell us if you know what that could be?" Honey prodded gently.

For a moment, Mrs. Harrington looked as if she might burst into tears to avoid answering the questions. Then she thought better of it and spoke instead.

"I am aware that Dick hasn't been quite himself lately," she said stiffly.

"'Not himself' is an understatement, my dear," said Mr. Harrington, coming into the drawing room.

"George, please!" Mrs. Harrington said sharply.

"My dear, James, with his friend Honey, has worked with police departments all over the Midwest, and even in Europe. His reputation as a young detective is beyond reproach. We need his help."

"Thank you, sir," said James.

"Not at all. I love my son, James. He's never been a model of deportment—we've spoiled him, I'm afraid. He's been getting into scrapes for a long while. But something has been troubling him lately. He's been off at all hours to meet someone, do something, I don't know who or what. Whatever it is, it hasn't seemed a happy experience. My feeling is, whatever it is has caught up with him. He wouldn't confide in me. But you're young, James. You can find out from the young people, from

Dick's friends, what I at my age can't. Please, help us find out what's been happening to our son."

"And please also, James, don't confide in the police. I don't want Police Chief Adams in on this," Mrs. Harrington said.

"Do you know or just suspect something underhanded in what Dick's been involved in, Mrs. Harrington?" James asked.

"I know nothing," said Dick's mother.

"What do you guess, then?" asked Honey, leaning forward to touch Mrs. Harrington's hand in comfort.

"I guess . . ." Mrs. Harrington began.

"Go on, my dear, it can't be helped. Whatever Dick's done in the past is over now. But unless we help now, he may never have a future," said Mr. Harrington.

"He once mentioned meeting a girl," Mrs. Harrington said awkwardly. "He mentioned going to meet her at Galaxy Games."

Galaxy Games was the video arcade half the kids at school hung around at least a couple of times a week.

"There's nothing so unusual about that," said James.

"Not the fact, no," said Mrs. Harrington. "But there was something about the way Dick mentioned it, as if there were something not quite right about the meeting."

"Will you investigate?" asked Mr. Harrington.

"We'll do our best," said James.

"And you'll keep our confidence?" asked Mrs. Harrington.

"From the police, yes," said James. "But I work for Sam Star. He'll have to have a complete report."

"Of course," said Mr. Harrington.

Sam would understand James's not meeting his plane at Loden Airport at four o'clock. Only a case would prevent James Budd from greeting Sam Star. And of course Sam Star understood about cases.

There were two things James noticed immediately upon entering the darkened interior of the Galaxy Games video arcade.

The first was that, considering the beautiful day outside, there were almost too many kids here, indoors, dropping their hard-earned chore money into the slots of the mechanical games.

The second thing James noticed was that they weren't laughing and talking over the noisy, flashing computer games as they normally did. They looked almost as robotically mechanical as the games they were playing.

CHAPTER SIX

Another Threat

As James and Honey moved slowly through the dim, cavelike game room with its electronic music and flickering lights, James noticed also the great number of relatively new additions to the rows of video games.

The newest addiction was to the small consoles that showed, for twenty-five cents, a twenty-minute movie. Some video screens had only one funnel viewer, like a slide viewer, so only one person at a time could watch the movie. Other console screens had four-sided viewing, for up to four persons.

"I hear some people don't go home for days," said Honey wryly.

"Are the movies any good?" James asked.

"I've only tried a couple," said Honey. "The science fiction and detective shorts aren't too bad. The dramas and love stories are awful."

"Must be, for you to say so," said James, "considering there's almost no movie too awful for you to enjoy."

He tugged her long hair teasingly. Then he remembered they were at the arcade on business.

The instant James saw Valentine, he knew she was the girl Dick Harrington had been coming here to meet. He knew it as surely as if he had asked. She had a watchful look.

"There," James said in a low voice. "Over there. She's it."

As she often did, Honey understood James without further explanation.

"Do you think they met for business or pleasure?" Honey spoke with a smile, so no one watching them would suspect she and James were there for anything other than pleasure themselves.

There was no point in scaring Valentine, who already seemed alert, ready to take off, before they'd had a chance to talk to her.

"If she has been meeting Dick, she certainly masked her concern for him when I was at her father's plant," whispered James.

"If she has any," said Honey. "It's possible Valentine has the name she does instead of, not because she has, a heart."

"It's the black leather — fools people every time," James returned Honey's joking.

A moment later, he was close enough to touch Valentine's shoulder. Honey disappeared into the shadows, knowing James would handle this better alone.

"Hello." James's low voice came close to Valentine's ear.

When she gave a small gasp, James added, "Budd. James Budd. Remember me?"

"James — what are you doing here?" said Valentine.

"Looking for you," said James, staying close. "I have a message. A message from Dick Harrington."

This time Valentine's gasp was louder. "Is he better? Can he go on? Or did he send you to take his place?" she whispered.

"Yes," said James. By playing along, he might find out even more than he'd hoped. The dark-haired girl covered James's hand with her own as she peered anxiously around the dark arcade, as if she wanted either not to be seen at all or not to be seen with him.

"Not here," she whispered. "I'll meet you tomorrow night. Eight o'clock at the usual place."

"The usual place?" James asked.

"Oh, sorry, of course you wouldn't know," said Valentine. "The usual place is the railway station. Go now. I'll see you tomorrow night."

An hour later, in their leather-and-brass living room, Sam Star put his feet up on the coffee table in front of the fireplace, pushed back his gray felt fedora, shoved his hands into his pockets, and asked James the same question Honey Mack had asked.

"What do you think, James? Were they meeting for business or pleasure?"

James smiled. "You ought to see her, Sam. Business or no business, it would be a pleasure to see Valentine."

"Do I get a complete report? Or do I get wisecracks?" A quick, affectionate smile lit Sam's sharp features. Then he yanked his tie loose from its moorings, opened his collar, and settled his bones to listen. "I'm tired of problems. I'm tired of reading the new reports about the terrorists I think they're going to put me onto next. I'm tired of almost everything I can think of, actually. Do you know what I need, James?"

"A week on the Kawabata farm," said James. "A week of Zen tea ceremonies, of hot tubs and massages, of meditation and chanting." James would have gone on to wax poetic about the curative powers of Zen relaxation techniques, but Sam interrupted him.

"Naw," said Sam. "A week of rest and I'd only end up chewing over the new case or my own navel. Naw, what I need is a different set of problems for a while. Tell you what. I'll make dinner while you give me your report. I want to hear about the Harringtons from the beginning, about your impressions of old man Wolf and the plant, and whatever else you think belongs in there."

The next hour was cozy. James and Sam enjoyed their bachelor privacy. In the kitchen, Sam broiled fish and James tossed a salad and warmed a loaf of French bread. Over dinner, James reported everything that had happened since Monday.

"Honey will have written the full report by tomorrow for the files," said James. "But so far, what do you think?"

"I agree with you, Dick Harrington was up to no good. And if he's been meeting this Wolf girl, she may also be up to no good."

"So you think they may be up to no good together?" said James. "In that case, it's just possible there's a connection between Mr. Wolf and his theft problems — and Dick Harrington and his problems."

"Smart thinking," said Sam. "But don't get too smart, James. Your life has been threatened twice already for coming too close. That means they think you know more than you think you know."

Sam Star was never wrong.

It was just after dawn, high on Kings Rock at the foot of Rock Bluffs, the private place northwest of town where James drove when he needed to be alone to think things through. A few moments after sunrise, a huge boulder came crashing down from the heights of the bluff above him, trapping James below.

CHAPTER SEVEN

New Girl in Class

The high outcrop of yellow rocks that jutted from Rock Bluffs at the foot of Nebraska's Sand Hills was called Kings Rock. The town had been named for it.

James could see Kings Rock from his bedroom window, hear the wind sweep and moan across it from the mountain pass. It had the color, the roar, and in bad weather the treachery of an angry lion, that king of beasts — hence its name.

It was James Budd's favorite place. Few people went there at all. No one ever followed him.

James went up from the prairies and into the hills that morning to think things out. The windswept rock, spare but for brush and scrub trees, cleared James's head. That morning, even the thermos of coffee and his tan suede jacket didn't keep him warm.

But when the dawn came up, spreading pink-gold flames across the empty sky, James rose to his feet and caught the answer he had been waiting for from the morning air.

He also nearly caught his death. The boulder hurtled down the rocky bluff above his head.

Golden Rule Number Three, thought James: *never say "never."* James liked "Golden Rules." He made up most of them as he went along.

Someone had followed him, even here. It was the same someone who had been wanting him dead all week.

"Blast him," yelled James.

As the huge rock came down, James quickly judged its path. What saved him was his knowledge of the bluffs. If he'd dodged the wrong way, he could have been caught in the rock's path or fallen into a crevasse in the sand hill bluffs. In a split second, James made his decision. He went over the edge of Kings Rock and hung on by his hands until the danger had passed. It was also a way of hiding the fact that he was still alive from his enemy.

That the enemy was familiar, James decided from the black chopper that picked the man up a few minutes later at the foot of the bluffs. Whoever was chasing James, whether in a car, on a motorcycle, or, as now, in a helicopter, preferred his metal black.

But the morning had given James his first answer. Volpone Wolf hadn't been nearly upset enough over the thefts. Nor had he yet mentioned any insurance agents, or his reasons for calling a private investigator rather than the police.

James suddenly understood why.

"He arranged for those parts to be stolen himself," said James to his car, when he returned to the Firebird he had parked at the foot of Rock Bluffs. "All I have to find out now is why he had the parts stolen, and by whom. Maybe Valentine will part with some information tonight."

The red Firebird didn't answer. But then, James hadn't expected it to.

Saturday mornings, James and his friends met at the Kawabata farm. Kobo Kawabata, Tad's father, made his living raising corn, feed crops, and dairy cows. He made himself and his friends happy by teaching them all Zen, from archery to tea ceremony, from martial arts to meditation. It was a whole new approach to life for Mr. Kawabata's students, including, for James, learning how to fold his long legs under him and sit on a floor, instead of dangling them, propped up on a chair.

"If you need a chair to sit on, a wall to lean against, will you then take these things wherever you go? Or will you learn, mind and body, not to depend?" said Kobo Kawabata.

As James drove back along Old Cattle Road to the Kawabata farm, he wondered about the connection between Dick Harrington and the Wolf family. One thing he knew for certain. Either Mr. Wolf or Mrs. Harrington was trying to have him killed because he knew of that connection.

James drove up the long, dusty farm road, past the red Nebraska barns, the silos, the vegetable gardens, to where the Kawabata family lived. Tad's father had built a Japanese home, a teahouse, heated baths, and a large meditation hall where he also conducted classes.

As James stepped, shoeless, onto the tatami, the Japanese straw matting that covered the floors, he bowed in greeting to the Zen master and then looked around. With relief, he saw that neither Honey nor Charlie was there for the Saturday morning class. That meant he could concentrate fully on the morning lessons.

The three of them — four, if Kathy Howard was there too — often communicated too much with each other, too little with their own work.

But as James stepped through the group to his own usual corner space, he spotted a new student.

What is she *doing here*? he wondered.

In the front row, in her white practice coat and trousers, was Valentine. She did not look at James as she sat cross-legged in meditation. She did not look at James during the fifteen-minute exercise session before their lesson in the arts of the "weaponless weapon" and the "empty hand" techniques, kung fu and karate. She did not look at James during Kobo Kawabata's reminder that these disciplines of the mind and body were only for awareness, for self-defense, not for attack — unless provoked. Most interesting of all to James, she did not look at James as she executed the iron elbow, the tiger claw, the sunfist, the snake fist.

Either Valentine hadn't seen him. Or she was trying to tell him something.

After all, Dick Harrington had been put away by a perfectly executed sunfist blow.

Before meeting Valentine, who had even left the meditation hall without a glance at him, James called Honey, Charlie, and Kathy. He wasn't sure what might happen that night. But he was sure he would want friends.

"Careful, James, she makes me nervous," said Honey on the telepone. Honey wanted to ride pillion.

"Shall I relay a message to the chief?" said Charlie on his end. Police Chief Frank Adams was always getting annoyed at James for withholding information.

"You need color?" Kathy demanded. "I'll raise an army."

James felt loved and protected. He still preferred, however, to go it alone to the meeting.

"There are things she might tell me she wouldn't tell a whole bunch," said James.

It was dark in the shadows behind the railroad station at eight o'clock that night.

"Is that you, James?" came a whisper.

"Yes, it's James," came the return.

The beautiful girl with the black hair emerged from the shadows.

"So Dick sent you to take his place for a while?" said Valentine softly. She looked up at James through her lashes. "I can't say I object."

James decided not to object either, until he found out what it meant to take Dick's place. What exactly was Dick's place?

Valentine kissed James.

So, thought James, *there is some pleasure involved.*

"Come on, now," Valentine said.

And there is business, too. But what?

CHAPTER EIGHT

Valentine
Haunts James

Valentine hadn't taken ten steps before James guessed where she was going.

"Don't tell me you're mixed up with Ratso Jones and those two creeps Tom and Sharky," said James.

Valentine continued to walk toward Ratso's run-down shack across the railroad tracks. "They may not be nice," she said. "But people like that can be useful sometimes, don't you think, James?"

"I agree that some shady characters can be interesting and useful," said James. "But I've had nothing but trouble from those three since we were little kids."

The moon hadn't risen yet. In the darkness, James heard the long, drawn-out call of a screech owl. Under his feet, he felt the first, faint, early-warning tremors of a train on the tracks.

"I feel like we're doing a bad scene out of an old movie," said James. "What are we going to find in the shack when we get there, Valentine?"

Valentine snuggled against James's shoulder as they approached the battered shack. Yellow cracks of light were visible in the small window and under the door.

"You'll see," was all Valentine would say on the subject.

But just before they opened the door to the shack, Valentine brought up another subject. "Do you think you could learn to like me, James?" she purred, lifting thickly fringed cat eyes to James's face.

Like her? No, James didn't like tricky women. Respond to her? *I'd have to be dead not to*, thought James. *But I'd have to be dead not to see also that I'm about to be used.* James smiled down at the vixenish girl.

"I might," he answered lightly.

Valentine pushed open the door.

A naked light bulb illuminated the starved, narrow-eyed rat face from which the gang leader got his name. He sat on a broken chair, hunched in his black leather jacket over a small, wooden table. Ratso's two sidekicks,

Tom and Sharky, hovered just behind his chair.

James knew their menace wasn't just a pose. He had seen the occasional results of their beatings down in Police Chief Adams's office, and, it was once suspected, in the city morgue.

"I told you not to bring him here."

Ratso's remark was addressed to Valentine. He sounded sullen, angry.

"I want you to trust him, Ratso," said Valentine, "just the way I wanted you to trust Dick Harrington, just in the same way, just to do the same things."

"We've never trusted each other yet, him and me. Right, Mr. James Budd?" said Ratso, his voice a sneer, yet wary, too.

So Ratso didn't want him here. Only Valentine wanted him in on whatever was going on.

And what was going on?

As James's eyes grew accustomed to the dimness in the corners of the room, he saw the answer.

There were piles upon piles of open boxes of electronics parts. The parts were exactly those Charlie had drawn, the parts Mr. Wolf had reported stolen, parts that when correctly assembled would form video cassette recorders, cathode ray tube screens, audio cassette recorders, and assorted assembly-unit parts. There were also piles of cassettes and filmstrip reels, as well as several boxes of complex installation equipment, electrical wire, and cables.

"We need someone people around here trust to help us sell the stuff, Ratso," said Valentine. "Do people around here trust you? They trusted Dick Harrington. They'll trust James Budd."

Valentine wasn't making an accusation, only a statement of fact. James watched Ratso Jones struggle between his greed and his hatred for James.

"What makes you think we can trust Budd, of all people?" said Ratso. "He works for a private eye. He's got friends down at the station. And he's not the kind to turn fence for us out of love for you, the way lover-boy Harrington did."

"Why not let me decide what I'll do and what I won't do," said James, "*and* the reasons for it."

"If we do tell you about the setup, how do we know you won't turn us in?" said Sharky.

Valentine crossed the floor to lean against

the wooden table. The black leather that covered her long legs matched the black leather jacket hunched over Ratso's shoulders. They were a menacing pair under the yellow light of the naked bulb that hung from the shack's ceiling.

"I don't work for the police," said James. "Valentine's father hired the Star Agency to locate some missing electronics parts. I've located them. Once he knows it's his daughter who's been arranging the thefts from his plant, I don't think he's going to press any charges. That saves your hide rather nicely, doesn't it, Ratso?"

Ratso sneered. "I always make sure my hide is protected," he said through curling lips. "That's why I'm alive so long."

"An interesting, if disagreeable, fact," said James.

He leaned casually against the doorjamb, one leg crossed neatly over the other.

"And now," said James, "bribe me. Tell me what the setup is, let me in on the action, and I'll delay my report long enough for you to get rid of the goods."

Valentine spoke quickly. *Too quickly?* James wondered.

"I've got copies of all my father's keys," said Valentine. "He trusts me. After hours, when the plant is closed, I let Ratso and the boys in. They take the parts they want, the parts they think we can sell. I let us out. I close the place up. We bring the stuff back here. We sell it. Dick was helping us sell the stuff smart, though, by the dozen, and to the right places. He'd walk into a shop and deal. He was so clean-cut everybody trusted him, trusted the stuff was clean. We'd been doing pretty good business till someone put him out."

"You have any idea who put Dick out of commission?" James asked.

Valentine shook her head. "Maybe someone guessed he was cleaning up and wanted in. Maybe he said no. Maybe whoever wanted in didn't like Dick's answer."

Again James wondered if Valentine's answers weren't too quick, too ready. James glanced at Ratso to see if the response was rehearsed. Ratso just sneered back at James as usual. No information on Ratso's face.

So James didn't question Valentine's theory just then. Another time, maybe, he'd have a chance to talk to her alone.

"So you want me to take Dick's place?" said James to the girl.

"She may, but I don't," said Ratso. "I don't trust you as far as I can throw you."

Like a snake suddenly striking, Ratso uncoiled and flung himself across the wooden table and onto James. He held a strip of rubber hose, raised to hurt. Behind him were his two thugs.

James Budd went down. The sound of a rattle was in his ears.

CHAPTER NINE

Mind Control

The rattle James heard was the sound of Charlie Alda's untuned car. And as James went down, so did the entire east wall of the shack. Charlie, Honey Mack, and Kathy Howard had flung themselves bodily upon it from the outside, until it collapsed itself inside the shack.

The battle was short. Honey and Kathy pinned Valentine to the dirt. Charlie and James simply grabbed Ratso Jones and threatened to wring his neck if Tom and Sharky didn't freeze.

"Shall we take these creeps in?" said Charlie.

"Or shall I just go for Sam while you hold them?" said Honey.

"Can I have the black leather pants while this person does her time?" said Kathy, astride Valentine and fingering the material.

James brushed dust from his favorite tweed jacket. He had just floored Ratso with a dragon-tail kick to the back of the legs, and was straightening up to bargain.

"James," Valentine called out sharply, before James had time to turn anybody or anything in.

Valentine's gleaming cat eyes smiled up at James, half hidden by the tangle of black hair and undaunted by her pinioned position.

"James," the voice came again, purring as little as a reminder of promises as yet unkept.

"Go on," said James.

"I promise Ratso will behave from now on. Is it a deal? Do we have a deal?" Valentine said persuasively.

James, victorious, smiled down at the girl.

"We have a deal," he said.

He took his foot from Ratso's back, nodded to Honey, and walked away.

When they were on a case, James and Honey never questioned each other in front of others. Honey got off Valentine instantly. Kathy followed suit. Keeping a watchful rear guard, Charlie was the last to back off.

True to Valentine's word, Ratso Jones and his boys made no further attempts to attack that night.

"I'll meet you later tonight," said Valentine, once again on her own two feet. She dusted herself off as the boys began to pick up the shack's east wall. "At the arcade? At Galaxy Games?" Then she added to James's retreating back, "And alone?"

"Tell," said Honey, as the four moved off down the railroad tracks. She touched James lightly on the cheek, to let him know how glad she was that he was all right.

He pressed her hand quickly, then spoke. "Valentine has been helping Ratso and his boys to steal parts from the Wolf Electronics Plant. She has her father's keys. The parts they steal, they stash in the shack. They make deals, then, with store owners, with private people, whoever they can, to sell the parts. Charlie, your drawings were so accurate I had no trouble identifying the components of video and audio recorders and their installation units, to say nothing of boxes of cassettes and cathode ray tubes. As for Dick Harrington, he was apparently their front man, being presentable and well known around town."

Honey Mack tossed her long silky mane and laughed. "When James recites like that, it usually means he doesn't believe half of what he's been told."

James grinned at his partner. "Smart girl. I not only don't believe half of it, I'm not even sure which half is the lie. Obviously, the parts are there. Obviously, they came from Volpone Wolf's plant. Obviously, the shack is just a halfway house. Obviously, Ratso and his boys are making some money out of this. As for the rest of Valentine's story, or lack of it, there are too many things left out. There was no mention of any threatening letter to me. There was no mention of my being chased by a black Chevy, a black motorcycle, or, this morning, a black helicopter. Valentine herself can't possibly need extra pocket money. And for the last piece of missing information, nobody seemed quite clear about what happened to Dick Harrington. One thing, however, is perfectly clear to me. Whoever delivered that kung fu blow to Dick's spleen, it wasn't Ratso Jones. I've seen the results of Ratso's beatings. He fights like a cave man, with rocks and clubs and sharp objects. He doesn't know a thing about martial arts."

"What now?" said Charlie. "Who can help now?"

"How does everybody feel about spending the evening at Galaxy Games?" said James.

"Yuck," said Kathy. "I have a date with

David Rivera. We *were* going to a *college* party, not a high school hangout. And I'm *not* dressed for an evening at —"

Kathy was still talking and protesting as she got into Charlie's car. They followed the other two in James's car across Station Road to Southbend Avenue, into Park Street, and north of town to the Galaxy Games arcade.

Before they went in, James said, "Listen, I know we've been playing this stuff for years, but please, pay a lot of attention to the games tonight. I don't know exactly what I'm looking for, but if you'll all talk while you're playing, I may hear something new that could help. Valentine hangs out here more than a girl like her should. The kids are coming here more than ever. I mean, look at them," said James as they entered the darkened hall. "Quarter after quarter after quarter, not only into the games, but into those new twenty-five-cent movie machines. I mean, it's been gorgeous out. But any afternoon you look, this place is packed. The playing fields have been practically empty, and nobody seems to have any energy left."

"Since when have you gotten moral about what people do?" said Charlie.

James shook his head. "It's got nothing to do

with morals. I don't care where people hang
their hats. What I'm wondering about is
whether the kids are actually choosing to be
here, to spend all their time and money here.
Something you said, Charlie, helped con-
vince me something's wrong in this place. It
was something you said about hypnotic sug-
gestion. When you described those missing
electronics parts, you didn't just say they
would assemble into a video cassette or audio
cassette recorder. You said some of the parts
could be used to send subliminal hypnotic
messages."

"So I did," Charlie agreed thoughtfully,
pushing his glasses up on his nose. "Okay,
let's go."

At night, Galaxy Games looked as much like
a disco as like an arcade. Disco music poured
from hidden speakers. Flashing lights and
spinning mirrored balls made one's head spin.
The hits, explosions, bleeps, and bells from
the games contributed to the outer-space sen-
sations. The arcade's owner had even been
clever enough to put in a pizza, candy, pop-
corn, and soft drink bar back in the corner.

"Amazing," said Kathy. "From here, you'd
never have to go home again."

"I think that may be the point," said James.

The four moved among the pinball, video game, and movie machines. They played a little of everything: Pac-Man, Missile Command, Space Invaders, Phoenix, Defender, Zaxxon, Pole Position, Galaga, Millipede, Dig Dug, Paragon, Time Warp. They saw two twenty-five-cent movies, and shared a pizza.

"Well?" said James.

"I don't believe how much money a rational human person can spend on a creature named Dig Dug so he can drop rocks on creatures named Pooka and Fygar," said Honey. "I feel silly and dazed and at the same time I want to go back and do it again."

"I couldn't agree with you more," said Kathy. "Why should a sane human person spend quarters on Dig Dug, when you could be spending the same money watching the Knight in Dragon Lair ramming his face into castle walls?" Kathy laughed, but she too felt dazed, and she too admitted that, silly as she felt, she wanted nothing more than to go back for more.

"Look at that," said James, suddenly angry.

He moved forward slowly so as not to frighten the child, and scooped a small, seven-year-old boy into his arms. The little boy, Jerry

Fine, had fallen asleep over the little table-top Pac-Man, his quarters gone, his endurance at an end.

Kathy knew Jerry's brother and took the boy from James's arms, to deliver Jerry to George Fine across the room at a Pole Position game.

"Charlie," said James in a low voice, "before Valentine gets here, I want you and me to examine the backs of these machines. You get my meaning?"

Charlie ran a hand through the thick blond curls. "Sadly, I do. I'm to risk life and limb, hoodlums and the police, to see if I can find any inserts that resemble the parts I drew and you saw in Ratso Jones's shack, from the list of Mr. Wolf's missing parts — any or all of the above. Am I right?"

"You are right," said James. "I apologize for the risk to your life and limb, but who else could I ask who has your knowledge of electronics?"

Even in the dark, Charlie could see James Budd's broad grin.

"Where shall we begin?" James asked.

"Yes," said Honey. "Which games have the best chance of being tampered with, and with what?"

Charlie explained some facts very briefly.

"The easiest ones to doctor would be the movies and the games like Dragon Lair, which are made from filmstrips and look like television sets. All you'd need to do is add a couple of frames on each filmstrip printed with words that said things like: PLAY MORE; PUT IN ANOTHER QUARTER; even, DON'T GO HOME or COME BACK TOMORROW. The eye wouldn't consciously pick those frames up because they'd move too fast. But the brain would catch the meaning through the eyes and might very likely obey, since the pleasure principle is being reinforced anyway — meaning, the words are only telling you what you want to do already, play the games."

"Awful," said Honey.

"Really," Charlie agreed. "Computer graphics are brighter and prettier than the film games, but they're pretty much limited to just sticks and lines and circles. They function in a totally different way from film games. You can't reprogram the computer right in the arcade, so you'd have to run a filmstrip behind the graphics, again using a couple of frames every few seconds to flash a message on the video screen. What you're looking for, feeling around the back of the machines for, are cassette recorders that hold the cassettes with the filmstrip messages."

"I feel as if we're fighting a sort of subliminal war," said Honey.

"We are," said James grimly. "Dick Harrington may be our first casualty, and for reasons we don't even know yet. Let's get going."

"We better get going," said Charlie. "You have a date with Valentine any minute and you're not supposed to have us around."

"I don't like leaving you alone with that girl," said Honey.

James kissed Honey fondly.

"I don't mean because of that," said Honey seriously. "I think she's dangerous, and I don't think I'm saying that for the wrong reasons."

"I understand," said James. "But this mind control war has to be stopped. Look at the robots around this room. They used to be our friends. And did you see little Jerry? That was no allowance he was spending. Jerry is out, rain, cold, or burning heat with his little shoeshine box, to earn that money he fell asleep spending."

"I know," said Honey.

She was used to James's fierce sense of protection, just as he was used to her nurturing.

"Just be careful, James," Honey added, as the four dispersed to examine, where and how they could, the video and movie machines in the dark womb of the arcade.

A few moments later, when Honey looked up to find James, he was gone.

The man dressed in black, who stood where James had just been, had exactly the same profile as the silhouette of the man who had left the note threatening James's life last Monday.

As Honey screamed, the man in black vanished as James had vanished. Both were just simply gone.

CHAPTER TEN

Partners in Crime

When James came to from a blow to the back of his head, he saw the cement walls and high, barred windows of a basement, and heard the voice of Volpone Wolf.

"Even if criminal investigation weren't the trade by which you pay your own way in life," said Mr. Wolf, "I suspect you haven't the gift of minding your own business."

"Sam says things like that," said James.

He rubbed the back of his throbbing head awkwardly. Awkwardly was the only way he could use his hands at all, since they were bound together in front of him.

"Sam is astute," said Mr. Wolf. The smile was white, wolfish, in the dark face, and the eyes under the overhanging brows did not smile at all. "You, however, are less astute, my young friend."

"I don't see how you figure that," said James. Bound hands notwithstanding, he got easily to his feet. "I've found your missing electronics parts."

"I know," said Volpone Wolf.

"You know where I found them?" James asked.

"Valentine came directly here to our apartment. She told me everything, how she and her friends stole the few little parts for resale," said Mr. Wolf. He smiled a sort of paternal smile. "She wanted extra pin money, for clothes, she said. She didn't want to bother me. She thought I wouldn't miss a few little things here and there. I've scolded her, of course. But I think, in her way, she was only trying to be a little enterprising. Sweet, don't you think? I mean, after all, her father's a bit of a pirate now and then, so that kind of pluck does run in the family."

James stared coldly at the man who had had him kidnapped. Either Mr. Wolf was stupider than James had thought and believed his daughter had told him the whole truth. Or Mr. Wolf thought James was stupid enough to believe Valentine's explanation and his own acceptance of it. Those missing parts weren't just bits and pieces Valentine was selling so she could buy more leather pants. Those parts added up to a whole production factory of loops, video tapes, cassette recorders, for the sole purpose of hypnotizing kids to put every quarter they could beg, borrow, or earn into those video games and movie machines. Somebody was getting very rich here, not just a new pair of pants.

The long look James Budd and Volpone Wolf exchanged was a draw. Neither learned the answers to his questions, neither got nor gave any information.

James would get nothing, yet, from the old man. But he wasn't through, yet, with the daughter.

"I had a date, you know, with Valentine," said James. "I'm not in the habit of standing up young ladies. So if you wouldn't mind releasing me . . ."

"What were you and your friends searching for in the arcade?" demanded Mr. Wolf, his tone suddenly harsh. "Answer this question, and you shall be released."

Why do you want to know? James thought.

Aloud, all he said was, "Just another place we thought we might find more missing parts.

After all, you'd given me a general list, but not exact numbers. There might have been other stashes besides Ratso Jones's shack."

Mr. Wolf weighed that.

Then he underestimated James, and let him go.

"Valentine is waiting at Galaxy Games. Go now," said Mr. Wolf. He blindfolded James, led him along some passages, up a flight of stone steps, and, opening a door, paused. He cut James's bonds with his pocket knife, and, removing the blindfold, let James go. The cool, dark night air touched James's face. He was free.

Kidnapping was big business. James knew Volpone Wolf knew that. There had to be some pretty powerful reasons the old fox didn't want James exploring Galaxy Games. Was it to protect his daughter Valentine? Was he himself involved in some way?

James felt that after he met Valentine, he'd better get hold of Sam, who might even want to have a talk with Police Chief Frank Adams.

Honey, who knew James Budd better than anyone in the world, watched him as he strode, straight and strong and determined, into Galaxy

Games an hour after he had disappeared. He was looking for Valentine Wolf, and Honey could see the anger under the quiet cool.

But as he strode forward into the dark, flashing interior of the game room, the anger became visible even to those who didn't know him so well.

"Valentine!"

James's voice called out above the explosive game sounds and arrested the girl. Valentine looked wildly around, and then sprang like a cat behind the pinging pinball machines and the black curtain beyond.

"Blast!" said James.

He wheeled around to see what had scared the girl off. There were Honey, Charlie, and Kathy to one side. There were Sam Star, Chief Adams, and two police officers on the other.

"What is everybody doing here?" James asked. "I've just lost my main line of information."

"You may remember," said Honey, "you were missing in action an hour ago. I thought you had been kidnapped. I thought I'd better call Sam. Sam thought he'd better call Chief Adams. And we all thought we had better start looking for your trail here, since here is where you were missing from. Can you fault my logic?"

"No," said James. His anger broke, anger directed at the Wolfs anyway, and not at Honey Mack.

"Mad at me?" said Honey.

"No," said James. He gave her a hug to prove his word. "I'll find Valentine later," he said.

"Later is right," said a voice behind James. "I want a word with you."

Frank Adams was big, dark, good-natured, and a good friend of Sam's. His voice was seconded by James's adoptive father.

"We both feel you've been holding out on us," said Sam, pushing his gray fedora back and grinning up at his tall son. "I'm sure Frank has a pot of coffee on at the station. And I feel sure we're invited."

"Do you need us any more tonight?" said Kathy, looking as much to Honey as to James in case support was needed. "Otherwise, since David has been waiting for three hours, and I have this divine new sweater on . . ."

"There's a late show at the Starlight Theater, if you don't need me," said Charlie.

"We don't," said James. "Thanks, both of

you," he added, and meant it. "I'd have been bloody without your crashing the party this evening."

"Bloody?" said Sam.

"What party?" Frank Adams demanded. "What evidence has that young assistant of yours been holding out on this time, Sam?"

Chief Adams found out most of James's story down at the station on High Street South behind City Hall. In his office, he and Sam, waving coffee mugs, questioned James and Honey. The only part James held back was the possibility of Dick Harrington's involvement. Any police questions at the hospital might provoke Dick's attackers to further attempts on Dick's life.

"So," said Frank Adams, summing up, "your feeling is that Valentine's traffic in those missing parts isn't as innocent as her just wanting to make some pin money."

"Right," said James. "My feeling is she's as much her father's partner in crime as Sam and I are partners in criminal investigation. I think that penny ante stuff going on in Ratso Jones's shack is a cover."

"It's something to look cute, while the real operation is going on somewhere else," said

Honey. "And I've seen Valentine, and she's cute all right."

James encircled Honey's waist with his arm. "Cute is as cute does. And the lady in black pants is as cute as a panther. Chief, could you make a couple of telephone calls for me? My theory is that Volpone Wolf is providing audio and video parts that flash hypnotic messages to the kids who play these games, to keep them coming back for more, to keep them spending every cent they've got playing video games. The kids are getting not only broke but kind of sick-looking, and that old man and his daughter are getting rich. Think you could find out who owns the Galaxy Games arcade? Then we could find out where the owner buys the machines, because whoever owns the machines is in business with Mr. Wolf."

Sam Star slouched back in his chair, grinning with pleasure at his adopted son's ability to get to the bottom of things. "Anything you need from me?" he asked.

James grinned back. "Not now, Sam, thanks."

"In that case, I have some paper work to do. And when you're through with this, James,

I'm going to need *your* help. Honey, can you come over tomorrow? I know it's Sunday, but you're the only one who can write up my reports so they make sense to me. Besides, I like your pretty face around to cheer up the odd Sunday afternoon."

Sam pulled his hat forward and rose to leave, saying to James in passing, "I feel sure I've taught you that you need evidence as well as theory?"

James removed an object from his pocket, one of the missing parts he had picked up from the shack floor when Ratso wasn't watching.

"I can prove the theft, at any rate," said James.

"He can prove more than that, Sam," said Frank Adams, getting off the telephone. "He can prove that not only does Mr. Volpone Wolf supply the video games personally to Galaxy Games, but he owns the arcade himself, and another dozen or so like it across the country. He's making some real money."

"He's making a blasted fortune," James exploded, "and out of the hides of my friends. And that little witch is helping him. They probably arranged those thefts between them to cover up Mr. Wolf's real activities, so he could look done to rather than the doer."

From the doorway, which he hadn't quite left, Sam Star said, "Remember the rest of the whodunit lesson, James?"

James climbed down from his anger and laughed. "Find out if there's a doer behind the doer," he said. "What's more, I have an idea how to find out, and from whom." He cocked his head at Chief Adams. "No charges for a couple of days, okay?"

"You got forty-eight hours," said the chief.

CHAPTER ELEVEN

The Black
Metal Menace

Not once during the slow ten-mile run along the Nebraska roads that stretched like white ribbons in the morning sunlight did James think about all the black metal that had been chasing him for a week. Some people looked over only their thoughts, their worries, their inner scenery, no matter where they were. James preferred to watch the outside world. It often saved his life, since he tended to notice things other people missed.

This Sunday morning, he noticed something toward the end of his run even he might have missed. It was almost completely hidden behind the enormous hydrangea bushes at the end of the alleyway behind the houses on High Street North.

"That black Chevy sedan is out there," said James.

Sam and Honey were sitting in the kitchen, in a pool of autumn sunlight. The sun flooded the room, brightened the white table and chairs, covered the Sunday papers.

James would have loved coming upon this brightness, if it weren't for the black metal menace down the back alley.

"It's parked just down from Charlie Alda's house," said James.

"The one we chased after the driver delivered the note threatening you with the same blow Dick Harrington got?" said Honey.

She looked up from the notes Sam had been dictating.

"The same," said James.

"Same driver?" said Honey.

"Unless there's someone hiding down low, the car looked empty," said James.

Sam Star rose to lead the investigation. He pushed back the gray felt hat, hitched up his pants, and held up one hand.

"Don't try to stop me," said Sam. "I know it's your case. I know Frank Adams gave you forty-eight hours before either he or I took action. But in the past week, you've been chased, attacked, hit on the head, and kidnapped. I've grown very fond of you, James, these past twelve years, and I'd like to see you get from sixteen to sixty, if it's all the same to you."

"Hear, hear!" said Honey, nodding with enthusiasm.

"Now I don't have to tell a crack investigator like you, James," Sam Star went on, "that a driverless black sedan in the alley parked three doors down behind your best friend's house has got to be a booby trap. Now do I? Do I, James?"

James laughed at Sam's banter. He also paid attention. Sam only bantered when he meant serious business.

"You have a plan?" said James.

"I do," said Sam solemnly. "The three of us will pick up a mug of coffee each and calmly walk out the back door. Just as if we were going to take a Sunday stroll on this lovely morning. Just as if we were going over to the Aldas' to have our coffee with neighbors. Friendly like, you see."

He picked up his coffee mug and, holding it aloft like a flag, began to lead the small parade.

"Then, as we get there," he continued, "I am going to peer into the car window. If my guess is right, nothing at all will happen."

"If your guess is wrong?" said James, following Sam.

"Next, after I have peered into the window and moved on, Honey will follow suit, peer into the window, remark loudly that she sees nothing, and pass on after me."

"Check," said Honey, following James.

"If your guess is wrong, Sam?" repeated James.

"Then, after Honey has peered into the window and moved on, you, James, will take your turn. You will, however, peer with a difference. The minute you have made the smallest peering movement, you will instantly, immediately, without drawing a single breath, fling your bones over the hedge into the Alda back yard. Understood?"

"Exactly," said James. He beamed his approval of Sam's plan.

"Smart son I got me," said Sam, beaming back.

"Could I get in on the beaming around here," said Honey, "or is it just a boy thing?"

"Beam and move it," said Sam. "We don't want anyone out there getting nervous too early. We've been spotted by now, I should think."

Sam moved out smartly, according to his plan. He peered in through the black sedan's window as if looking for a driver, as if looking the car over, very casually.

Honey, not yet certain what this charade was about, did the same. As Sam moved another few steps down the alleyway and into the Aldas' yard, Honey peered in through the window, seemed to examine the upholstery and the dashboard, and followed Sam into the yard.

James was next.

"Silly business," said Honey, "for a Sunday morning."

"Silly, indeed," muttered Sam.

James pushed his *self* into a kind of inner locked drawer, as he always did when facing personal danger. He could then proceed freely without being too troubled by fear for that self. It was a necessary procedure in the next few seconds.

He followed in Sam's and Honey's footsteps, knowing that for him there was a difference.

He moved toward the black sedan with caution. He paused at its front fender. He put his head briefly through its window, seeming to examine its dashboard.

Then he leaped away and threw himself over the hedge. Sam and Honey were already ducked down. James ducked beside them. His dark hair had just touched the gray and the honey blond of his favorite heads, when the boom of the explosion cracked in the alleyway. Pieces of black sedan flew high and rained down everywhere.

After the Aldas and half a dozen other neighbors had put out the fire, they all naturally looked to Sam, James, and Honey for an explanation.

"Tried to kill James," said Sam cheerfully. "Remote-control switch. No point in chasing the man. He'll have gotten away by now."

When the neighborhood people continued to express their shock and fear in the aftermath of the explosion, Sam said, "Nobody hurt, right? James is alive, right? Sorry for the alarm, folks. Have a nice day."

James shook his head ruefully. Sam never could understand why people made such a fuss if they'd come out all right. Sam had made sure everyone was out of the way first, hadn't he? Well, then. No need to carry on.

James watched Honey moving among them

all, soothing and calming less stoic tempera-
ments.

"Matter of fact," said Mr. Alda, a stoic like
Sam, "I'm glad you're here. Charlie's looking
a bit peaked this morning."

"Charlie?" said James. "What's the matter
with Charlie?"

"Don't know," said Mr. Alda. "He's shaky,
pale, weak, says he feels dizzy and upset at his
stomach. He's in there, James, in the lab," Mr.
Alda added, pointing to a small shed at the
side of the yard.

Mr. Alda was a builder. When Charlie ex-
pressed his need for a laboratory separate
from the house to use for experiments, Mr.
Alda had built Charlie one of his own design.
The two were close. Mr. Alda seemed worried
now.

James and Honey crossed the yard to visit
their friend. He lay on an old cot along the far
wall of the shed.

"Your dad's right," said James. "What is it,
Charlie? You look awful."

CHAPTER TWELVE

The Challenge

When Dr. Grayson Howard, Kathy's father and doctor to most of Kings Rock, had examined Charlie Alda, he sighed deeply.

"I've seen Charlie's symptoms all over town," he said. "It seems to be going through our young population like the flu. Tremors, loss of strength, dizziness, nausea, the pale, glazed look with the loss of ability to concentrate — some doctors are beginning to call it computer syndrome. It's a brand-new affliction, brought on by too much video screen exposure. People whose jobs require too much time in front of computers and kids who spend too much time in front of video games are the ones suffering the most." He looked down at Charlie. "It's the absolute worst in the kids, though. They focus so hard on those games, and the graphics move so quickly. The eyestrain is terrific." Dr. Howard shook his head. "Wish we could pass a law limiting exposure time."

"I wish we could pass a law limiting people who tamper with those games to a few square feet in a prison yard," said James grimly.

He bent over his friend. Charlie smiled weakly up at him.

"What were you doing last night, Charlie?" asked James. "What I think?"

"What do you think?" said Charlie.

"I think you were testing out the games at the arcade. I think you were doing some research on my behalf," said James.

"I didn't intend the research to go on so long," said Charlie. "I really did feel hypnotized, like I couldn't stop playing. I must have been at Galaxy Games till it closed."

Sam raised a questioning eyebrow.

"Galaxy Games stays open till four o'clock in the morning," said James.

"Long night," said Sam.

"Nonstop playing for five hours will get to you," Charlie admitted. "And you know what? Bad as I feel, something's tugging at me to go back and play some more. No question in my mind about the doctored video screens."

"You stay put," said James. "Honey and I will take care of what has to be done."

"Not without either my own or a police escort, you won't," said Sam Star. He snapped his fedora brim into place. "That last attempt on your life was major. It means they're really keeping an eye on you, and their eye wants you in very bad health. Also, that car blowing up may have been meant only for you, but it could have taken some other people as well. You're a walking death rattle, James. You need protection, and people need protection from you."

That was a long speech for Sam. It meant he was worried.

James protested anyway. "Frank Adams gave me forty-eight hours. That gives me until tomorrow night," he said. "Not that I'm not grateful for your offer. It's just that I think someone my age would be less obvious at Galaxy Games than a police chief and a nationally famous private investigator."

"You have a point," agreed Sam grudgingly. "Have you also a plan?"

"Whatever it is, I'm coming along," said Charlie.

"Whatever it is, Frank Adams and I will be hovering," said Sam.

"No to both of you," said James. "You're not well, Charlie. And Sam, you and the chief would only call attention to what I'll be trying to do, even if you're only hovering."

Honey held James's arm in an iron grip. "Try and leave *me* behind, and you'll wind up with a broken bicep from a girl hanging from your left elbow."

"Would I leave you?" James asked sweetly.

He and Honey left the Aldas, Charlie, and Sam Star and Dr. Howard and Band-Aid too quickly for further questions.

"*Have* you got a plan?" said Honey.

"First, warmer clothes and a picnic lunch. Then the art show on the Green. Then maybe a ride out to the Kawabata farm, have a bowl of tea. Then if the afternoon is still lovely —"

"James," Honey prodded, "what's the plan?"

"First, warmer clothes and a picnic —"

"I heard that part," said Honey.

"Well, there's nothing I want to start until

dark," said James. "But why waste a terrific Sunday afternoon?"

There was more to it than that, Honey knew, because Honey knew James Budd's habits. One of them was to clear his mind before any major action.

"A full mind can be full only of the past," Mr. Kawabata often said. "Only an empty mind is open to the new."

An hour later, James stretched out in the dappling sunlight not far from the old-fashioned white lacy bandstand on the Kings Rock Green. He watched as Honey Mack careened toward him on the blue Honda. She had dressed as he'd asked her to, in clothes to match his own — jeans, a black turtleneck sweater, leather gloves, a dark down jacket.

"A little warm, these clothes," she said, dropping down on the soft grass beside James.

"They won't be, later. And they're dark. And you'll need the gloves," said James. "For now, though, take the gloves off and eat."

James had provided the lunch, a basket full of cold chicken, hard-boiled eggs, crusty rolls, half a chocolate cake, and a thermos of tea. There was a small white linen tablecloth and napkins.

"Gorgeous, James," sighed Honey.

"You're a better driver than I am," said James cheerfully. "I don't see why I shouldn't be a better cook." James served them both. "Now relax and enjoy the afternoon."

After lunch, James and Honey joined other Sunday afternoon strollers as they took in the paintings on exhibit at the outdoor art show. Then, leaving Honey's Honda parked under its tree, they climbed into James's red car and drove out to the Kawabata farm.

James spent half an hour in the meditation hall, sitting on his black cushion, exploring his relationship with himself. Then he spent an hour among the animals, and joined Mr. Kawabata and Honey in the small teahouse, exploring his relationship with everything else under the heavens.

By six o'clock, James felt emptied out. There were no leftover thoughts or problems to upset his head, and he was ready to function clearly.

He and Honey bowed to Mr. Kawabata, who bowed and smiled in return. No words had passed on any serious subject. No words were necessary.

By seven o'clock, James had dug out a sizable hole in the side of the bluff overlooking Kings Rock.

By eight o'clock, James and Honey had entered the darkness of Galaxy Games.

Above the crashing explosions, sonic zooms, and clanging bells of a couple of dozen video games, James could hear his Honey's voice ring out, loud and clear for everyone present to understand. Then, in case she had missed anyone, Honey's voice rang out her message again.

"Valentine! Valentine Wolf, I want your hair, and I want it out by the roots. How dare you mess around with James Budd!"

Even the robotlike players turned around to watch, as they heard Valentine's answering yowl.

"And how dare you question me! James Budd is mine now, not yours."

Valentine Wolf, her black hair shining in the flashing colored lights, her black leather pants tight above her boots, leaped into the center lights of the room. Her legs were bent and apart like a springing cat's, her hands in a position familiar to James, with the right straight out, the left hand at the right elbow.

Valentine was prepared for the sunfist fight — the blow that had felled Dick Harrington. Why hadn't James thought of it? Honey would have called it his chauvinist thinking, not considering that a female might have knocked Dick nearly to heaven. But Valentine, too, had been to their martial arts classes, and was obviously previously trained.

James watched the two girls circling each other another moment or two before he moved off. He smiled. Honey was getting set for that whipping hook kick of hers. Valentine Wolf had met more than her match.

The first part of James's plan was working. Honey's mating challenge, or whatever they called it in the jungle, was working. All James needed was five or ten minutes with everyone's attention off him and on the girls.

In the inside pockets of his black down jacket, James had placed whatever tools he thought he'd need. Now, slipping past the crowds without being noticed, he disconnected one of the video games in a far corner. Crouching down behind it, he set to work. Charlie's tools, especially designed to fit James's needs, were perfect.

The small, laser-bright flashlight was clipped to James's arm strap. It moved with his hand, shedding light exactly where it was needed. A tube constructed like a fountain pen held hydrochloric acid strong enough to corrode and melt most metals. There was also, among other things, a small, battery-powered drill.

James had the back of the video game off in no time. There was what he'd hoped to find, luckily on the first go. It was a small video recorder, complete with the programmed tape, numbered and traceable to the parent factory.

Within five minutes, James had attacked and opened three more video games, and emptied each one of similar parts.

James and Honey each wore a watch, Charlie-rigged so they could buzz each other. James hoped that Honey could hear her watch buzz above the yells of the crowd, and that Valentine hadn't pulled the watch off in a wrist grip.

Any moment, the kids would be pulled hypnotically back to their games. Not much else these days held their attention for long. James packed the four sets of components into a black nylon sack, put the precious tools back in his inside pockets, and buzzed Honey a second time. On the third buzz, Honey was to duck under Valentine's attack and race to the back door of the arcade. The red Firebird was parked just behind.

James heard the crowd yell louder. Who had been hurt? He knew their friends wouldn't let Valentine do any real injury to Honey, if Valentine should somehow prove the cleverer fighter of the two.

But he also hoped Honey could get loose. They had only a few minutes to get those parts hidden in the hole above Kings Rock, before a hunt was begun. The kids, returning to their machines, would notice four of them broken into and damaged. Valentine would know exactly what had happened and whom to look for. Whether she called the Rat Gang or her father and his goons or all of them was a moot point.

What *was* the point, was to get out. Without a head start, James would never make it to the bluffs with the equipment. And without the equipment, he didn't have a case. He didn't want the stuff taken from him after all the work he'd done to get it. Besides, the damage he'd caused would alert Mr. Volpone Wolf. The old man might just dismantle Galaxy Games himself, in order not to be caught. He'd just set the whole thing up in another town and another, reaping young people's money like wheat.

All this went rapidly through James's mind as he crept to the back of the arcade and opened the door.

James took a deep breath. Then he buzzed Honey for the third and last time.

CHAPTER THIRTEEN

Rescue by Moonlight

James crouched in the shadows just outside the back door, listening to his imagination. He ran it like a movie, listening to and watching what must be happening inside the arcade.

"Get her, Ratso, she's running out," Valentine's voice screamed above the crowd.

"Never mind her," Ratso's voice howled back. "It's Budd me and the boys are looking for. It's him could cause us trouble, not her. She's the decoy. Betcha he's already hit pay dirt and scrammed."

"Watch out, you zombies," Valentine's voice shouted back.

You helped your father make mechanical toys out of human beings, and you dare to call them names! James thought angrily. But the way to get Valentine was not to waste time on her now. The way to get Valentine and

Volpone Wolf was to get out of here with the video recorders and cassettes, and hide them up in the bluffs until their numbers could be traced. Then Wolf could burn the whole place down, and James could still prove his case.

But Ratso Jones and his boys would come out that back door in a minute, to go over the parking lot.

"Honey!" James whispered into the darkness. "Get a move on!"

"Come on, James, what are you waiting for?" The whispered call came flying back at him, as Honey herself came flying through the door.

James followed the fastest legs in Kings Rock across the lot to the Firebird. Honey had the car revved up before James had his door closed. At a speed James didn't want to know about, Honey took North Loup River Road above Kings Rock, to circle across to Rock Bluffs. The moon was still low. She pulled up in the shadows of the foothills.

"I know I haven't died and gone to car-crash heaven," said James. "I can hear my own voice."

"Very funny," said Honey. She piled the long, shining hair high on her head and pulled on a navy watch cap. Nothing could catch a glint of light from either of them now. "You want help carrying something?"

"I'll carry the bag. You grab the shovel," said James.

They were off. Up the bluffs they went, using the small paths they both knew so well. The climb up Kings Rock took only ten minutes in daylight. By night, with no moonlight, it was a bit slower.

Fifteen minutes later, they were in front of the eye-level cleft they had made earlier that day in the bluff overhanging Kings Rock. James strapped the laser-bright torch to his arm again, took the shovel, widened the hole slightly, and hoisted the black nylon bag.

As he passed the shovel back to Honey and pushed the bag of video components into place, two things happened simultaneously.

The moon rose high enough to light up Kings Rock. And the sound of motors could be heard faintly over the prairie.

"They're coming after us, Honey," said James. "What's more, they can see us."

"Next time make arrangements with the moon, all-powerful one," said Honey.

"Now who's being funny," said James. "Come on, quick."

Moon and motors or no moon and motors,

they had to get that bag hidden, covered over. Racing with time, the two used gloved hands to pile and shove the dirt they had removed earlier back into the hole, now half filled with the black bag. In a few minutes, it was all covered over. James concealed the mouth of the hole with a rock, while Honey scuffed to hide the newly dug dirt.

The moon grew higher and brighter. The hum of the motors grew closer and louder.

James now knew what the motors were. One was a heavy-duty motorcycle, coming up Old Cattle Road. The other was a chopper, coming down from the airport. All he didn't know was who was behind the motors.

"We do know who is behind whoever's behind the motors," said James.

"That gives me I can't tell you how much comfort," said Honey.

"Would you care to get out of here?" said James.

"Fast," said Honey.

By daylight, the trip down from Kings Rock took seven minutes. By night, it took eight minutes. That night it took three minutes. But they never made it to the car.

The black helicopter dipped and hovered

and swirled its choppers to back James and Honey away from their escape. The roar was too deafening for James and Honey to hear each other yell. But they had both been on enough cases and chases with Sam to know what was happening.

The black helicopter was trapping them until the person on the motorcycle arrived to take over.

As James and Honey kept trying to fight their way through the dust and the swirling air and the whirring movements of the machine, the motorcycle appeared, large, black, and menacing. The bike pulled up right beside Honey, and its rider pulled Honey in close.

As the helicopter rose a little to give the rider room to maneuver and speak, the rider, face hidden under his black helmet, shouted two sentences only.

"Get the stuff, Budd. I've got the girl."

"You give me the girl, you get the stuff. Otherwise, no deal."

There was nothing to argue with in James Budd's steely tone.

The rider released Honey. Honey ran to James. The two started back up Rock Bluffs.

"I'm counting on the fact that they don't

know, can't have seen, the exact place," said James. "What we're going to do is just keep on climbing the bluffs."

They climbed at the normal rate for the first few minutes. Then they speeded up. The rider climbed behind them, the helicopter hovered nearby.

"Keep climbing," urged James, protectively just behind Honey.

"There isn't any farther up to go," said Honey, "only across the rock table."

"Go across," said James.

The two of them, dark figures outlined in the moonlight, raced across the open rock table toward the Sand Hills beyond.

The helicopter pilot got it. He realized they weren't going after the stolen parts. He realized they were just going. He didn't like it.

"He's coming down on us," shouted James. "Flatten out, Honey. Flatten as out as you can get."

The two of them threw themselves face down on the rock.

"Now crawl," shouted James. "Follow me, and keep crawling."

James lifted his head just a second to look behind them. The rider had crawled over the bluff ledge, had spotted them, and was racing across the rock table. The helicopter was pinning them to the ground so they could barely crawl.

James thought he heard a roaring in his ears as he flung his body over Honey's and pulled her along with him the few more feet toward a pile of boulders.

James had just flung Honey to safety when the roaring increased. He pivoted quickly to take on the black-helmeted rider at the very least when the roaring rose to a deafening clatter.

James looked up.

A second helicopter had arrived, glinting large and blue in the moonlight. As it gave battle to James's attackers, James caught sight of a gray fedora. The fedora waved cheerfully at him from Sam's extended hand.

CHAPTER FOURTEEN

The Game Is Done

The body beside the Harrington pool seemed dead.

"James," said Mrs. Harrington. "Tell Dick to turn around. He'll get all sunburned on one side."

James Budd adjusted an umbrella over Dick, now finally recovering nicely after the surgery to remove his damaged spleen. Then he adjusted Dick's chair.

"Gently," said Dick. "I'm still not what you'd call a well man."

But Dick was smiling, glad to be alive in the golden, unseasonably warm afternoon of that Monday in a November he would never forget. For the first time in months, all was well with him.

"I have my scars, you know," he said, half jokingly.

James could see that his friend was still in some pain. There was still the physical pain left from the operation. There was also the pain of what he had done for love of Valentine, and what she had done back to him.

"That'll teach you to fall in love with female desperadoes," said Sam Star.

Sam was sitting with Mr. and Mrs. Harrington and Police Chief Frank Adams on the patio. He smiled over at James and Honey, Charlie, Kathy, and Dick, who were sprawled on lawn chairs near the pool. They had all come over to welcome Dick home, and to celebrate the close of the *Galaxy Games Mystery*.

"I couldn't believe it, when Valentine did that kung fu thing to me," said Dick. "It was bad enough all those months, peddling the stuff she and the Rat Gang collected from the Wolf Electronics Plant. I had even offered to give Valentine clothes money myself, if that was what she wanted, rather than act as front man for those stolen recorders and tapes."

"That would have been fine, if clothes money was really all Valentine wanted," said James. "But using you and Ratso and his boys to fence stolen parts was just a front she and her father had put together to cover what was really going on. Then Mr. Wolf could play innocent about the real and much larger movement of recorders and doctored tapes to Galaxy Games and the other arcades he owns. That was where the real money could be had — using those special recorders and tapes to hypnotize money out of young people wherever they played video games."

"I still can't believe that girl tried to kill me," said Dick. "I know I was dumb to fall for a pair of green eyes and all that gorgeous dark hair. And I know it was dumb of me just to tell her point blank I didn't want to be her front man any more, I just wanted her to love me for myself. But wow, I never thought she'd hate me enough to want me dead."

"I don't think she has enough emotion in her to hate," said Honey. "She says she just wanted to stun you, Dick, not kill, that your ruptured spleen was an accidental result of using the sunfist blow too hard. I talked to her after she was arrested. I believe her. I think she's spent a whole lifetime obeying that dreadful father of hers. I think she just does what she's told. I think, now that her father's going to jail, that if Valentine just had a good home —"

James stroked the long, honey-blond hair.

"That's my Honey," said James. " 'Adopt a stray a day' is her motto."

Honey giggled before she went on speaking. "She's not even good at martial arts techniques," she said. "I had to help make her look good to keep her fighting long enough to let you get away last night, long enough to wait until you buzzed Charlie's watch buzzer for me."

James nodded to his scientifically brilliant friend. "All that stuff worked just fine, Charlie. Thanks."

Charlie peered through his glasses and shook his curly head shyly. He was much recovered himself from the eyestrain and weakness of the day before. "So what exactly happened when the helicopters collided?"

"Well," said James, "there sure wasn't a doubt that the goons wanted me dead. What I had seen of your injury, Dick, the lists and recorder designs I'd seen on the factory wall, what I had seen on Ratso's shack floor, what Valentine had told me — all that made Volpone Wolf want me real dead. So when, on top of that, they knew that I had put it all together enough to raid the machines at Galaxy Games, they were covering the place, just waiting."

"And Frank Adams and I had put it together that Wolf and his men had put it together, so we were waiting, too," said Sam. "We not only have a larger helicopter attached to the Kings Rock Police Department, we have the Kings Rock police behind it."

"The guys beat it," said James. "When they saw the white star on the blue chopper, the black helicopter took off in one direction, and the black motorcycle took off in another."

"When we got to the plant to pick up Mr. Wolf, he had only one goon left, besides his daughter Valentine," Sam added. "We've closed the plant and arrested half a dozen of Wolf's men across the country who were involved with his national arcade syndicate. There may be more."

"You mean," said Kathy Howard, "there might still be video game arcades all over the country with hypnotic tapes getting kids' quarters out of them and conning them back for more play?"

"That's what I mean," said Sam. "With a man like Wolf, we may never get at the whole list."

"You mean he might still get rich off the kids?" said Honey.

"Might," said Sam. "But he'll also get ten

years for a list of assorted assaults, felonies, and tax evasion — to say nothing of James's and my bill."

"That's right," said James. "He asked us to find the missing parts. We found them. He got caught in time to pay his own bill before he, who paid for himself to be caught, gets sent to jail."

Sam Star whistled, long and low, under the gray fedora. "I sure didn't say that. I'm not even sure I could."

James Budd smiled in satisfaction. He stretched out in his chair, long and lazy, his dark, good-looking profile turned to the sky, his girl and his iced Perrier beside him.

Sam Star rose and wandered over to stand next to James.

"Comfy?" asked Sam.

"Comfy," said James.

"You deserve a rest," said Sam.

"I do," agreed James.

"Well, you're not going to get it," said Sam.

"I'm not?" said James.

Sam reached into his pocket and pulled out an envelope. An airline ticket wafted down into the lap of his partner and adopted son.

"That's for London, plane leaving Loden

Airport Friday after school," said Sam. "There's something I need you to do on this terrorist case, this *Secret of the Circus of Terror* I'm working on. Meet you there Saturday morning. There'll be a limousine at Heathrow Airport. Pick you up and bring you to wherever I am. I'm taking off now. See you then."

James watched as Sam sauntered off. The gray fedora waved once as it disappeared around the front of the Harrington mansion. James waved back.

"Why did you wave, James, when Sam never even turned around?" Honey asked thoughtfully.

"Only man I ever knew with eyes like that," said James. "Sees in every direction at once."

Without looking, James gave Honey's upturned face a very accurate kiss.

"Like father," said Honey, "like adopted son."

ABOUT THE AUTHOR

Dale Carlson has been writing stories since she was eight years old. She is the author of more than forty books for young people, including three ALA Notable Books: *The Mountain of Truth*, *The Human Apes*, and *Girls Are Equal Too*. Her book *Where's Your Head* won a Christopher Award.

Ms. Carlson lives in New York City.

THE JAMES BUDD MYSTERIES

1. **The Mystery of the Madman at Cornwall Crag**
2. **The Secret of Operation Brain**
3. **The Mystery of the Lost Princess**
4. **The Mystery of Galaxy Games**